Hello I am Amaya I can be found on twitter @youngmaı

I am 8 years old and have Autism, I struggle with the wo
home schooled as I couldn't cope with the school environment. I have a support
dog named Boo. She helps me to be able to cope in the world.

I am very passionate about marine life and want to be a marine biologist when I
grow up. I go on beach clean ups most days. So I see what people leave and do
to sea creatures e.g hurting jellyfish that are beached on the sand. I have had a
save the beach poster made into postcards on sale at sealife with the money
being donated to them.

I wanted to make this book to teach everyone that they should look after our
beaches and the creatures in the ocean. Also to teach people how we need to
help the planet and stop climate change. I think if one person reads this and it
makes them change how they are on the beach then I have achieved something.

I hope that this will then become a series of books to show how different places
are being effective and what can be done to help them.

I love sealife trust and all the work they do for our oceans and creatures in it. I
will be donating 10% of the sale off this book to them.

Hope you enjoy reading it.

Sun

Boo

House

Boo

Hello, I am Boo the dog.

I like to go on adventures and find out why we should help the planet.

Why don't you come and join me? I'm off on an adventure to the beach.

Frisbee

Wipe

Ball

Can

Carton

Bottle

Poo bag

Bucket

Spade

We are at the beach and it is a sunny day. "Look at all this rubbish" says Boo's owner. She asks Boo "how will all this rubbish affect the ocean and animals?"

Boo says "this sounds like an adventure, I will go and find out how."

Boo

Jellyfish

Fish

Rockpool

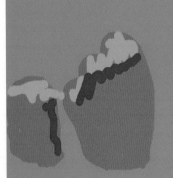

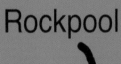

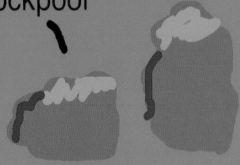

Boo dives into the sea to see what she can find out.

"Wow look at how many animals are in the ocean, its amazing and beautiful" says Boo.

"Look there is a rock pool, let's go explore" she says.

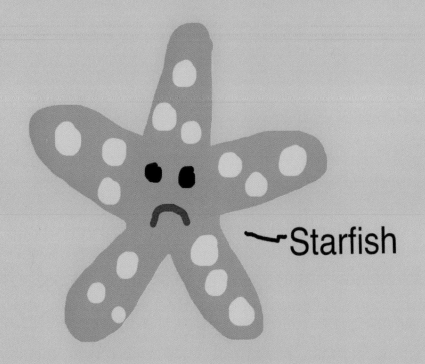

~Starfish

Mussel

Sea anemone

Crab

I can see starfish, sea anemones, crabs and mussels. They look upset.

Boo goes over to find out what is wrong. The starfish says "people have left rubbish on the beach which has come in the sea. This has trapped us in the rock pools and has stopped us from getting the sunlight."

The animals in the rock pool say "other sea animals are upset with the rubbish too." Boo says "I will go and find out why?"

Boo carries on swimming in the ocean and sees some seals. "Hi what are you up to?" asks Boo.

"We are upset as we were playing with these frisbees but now they are stuck around our necks." The seal then says "if we cannot get it off it will cause us serious harm."

Boo agrees that the frisbees should not be left on the beach as they get washed into the ocean. Boo then goes off to see what else is affected.

Micro plastic

Dolphin

Fish

Boo sees a dolphin in distress. She goes over to see what is wrong. "I've eaten some plastic and it has hurt my stomach" says the dolphin. "Also my pod ate fish that had toxins from plastic and it made them ill."

Boo says "that is really not good, something needs to be done." She goes to find out how it affects more animals.

Turtle

Plastic bag

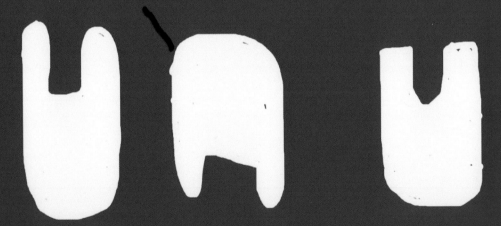

Boo carries on swimming when she suddenly sees a turtle. It looks upset so she goes to have a look.

"What's wrong?" asks Boo. "I thought I saw a jellyfish so ate it but it was a plastic bag" says the turtle. "The plastic has blocked my stomach" cries the turtle.

"Oh no" says Boo. She wonders if more animals are being affected.

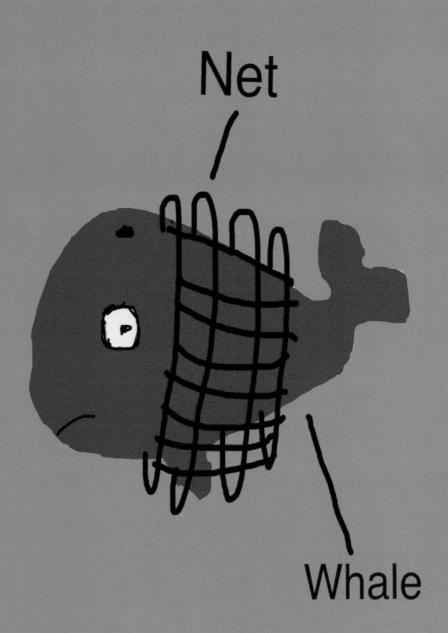

Boo swims further into the ocean. She sees a whale and goes to talk to it.

"Hello whale how are you?" asks Boo. "I am scared as I was swimming and got trapped in this net" the whale says. "I cannot get out of the net and I'm struggling to breathe."

Boo says "I will go and get help."

Boo swims back to the beach. She sees her owner and tells her about all the animals needing urgent help.

Boo's owner calls for help. Whilst waiting, Boo tells her all about the sea animals in distress and how human pollution has caused it.

Listening about all the animals being hurt by human rubbish upsets Boo's owner.

Boo's owner says "when you were finding out about the rubbish in the ocean, I found all these little plastic balls in the sand."

She goes on to say "I looked up what they are and they are nurdles. It is what all plastic is made from."

She then explains that they are put in the ocean when bags split on boats shipping them or that they get into rivers that then connect to oceans.

Boo says "that these will be causing damage to sea animals as they digest them and they will affect animals on the beach."

Save the beach

Help the sealife

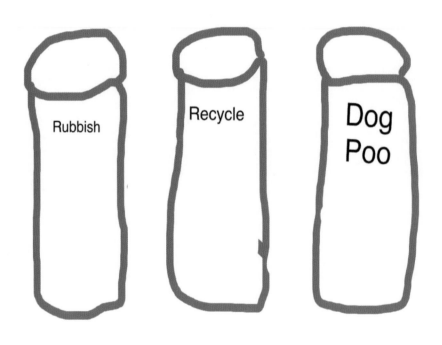

Put your rubbish in the correct bin

Boo's owner asks her "with what you have found out what should everyone be doing to save the ocean?"

Boo says "that all humans can save the ocean by doing the following things:"

- Take any rubbish they bring to the beach home or put it in the correct bin.
- Use frisbees that don't have a hole in the middle.
- If they see any rubbish on the beach pick it up.
- Make other people aware of the affect rubbish has on the ocean animals.
- Fishermen should take any broken nets or lines with them and not leave them in the ocean or on the beach.
- If they see an animal in danger call for help.

Boo finishes by saying "doing these simple things will help save our oceans and sea animals."

Please don't hurt
the jellyfish

Don't think they are dead
carefully put them in the water

They are important to
the ecosystem

Quiz

1 Which animal did Boo speak to first?
A) Dolphin
B) Starfish
C) Seal

2 How was the dolphin injured?
A) Eaten some plastic
B) Stuck in fishing line
C) Got a frisbee stuck round neck

3 What can we do to help the ocean?
A) Leave rubbish on the beach
B) Take rubbish with us or put in bin
C) Throw rubbish into the sea

4 What are nurdles?
A) Food you can eat
B) Jellyfish
C) What plastic is made from

5 What animal is Boo?
A) Dog
B) Cat
C)Dolphin

Answers: 1)B 2)A 3)B 4)C 5)A

Boo wants to thank you for reading this book. She looks forward to seeing you on her next adventure.

Printed in Great Britain
by Amazon